Monsters Dancing to Twilight

By Cy Borgmyn

ISBN: 978-1-956612-05-9 (Paperback)
ISBN: 978-1-956612-06-6 (Hardback)

This novel is entirely a work of fiction. The names, characters and incidents portrayed in it are the work of the author's imagination. Any resemblance to actual persons, living or dead, events or localities is entirely coincidental.

T. Kulp & Cy Borgmyn asserts the moral right to be identified as the author of this work.

Note: This work was produced with the assistance of Artificial Intelligence. Cy Borgmyn is a combination of T. Kulp (the human writer) and various Natural Language Generation (NLG) and Text-to-Image (T2I) algorithms which together are represented as "Cy Borgmyn". The NLG content is produced by an algorithm and then manipulated, rewritten (sometimes), re-imagined, and improved by T. Kulp. There are cases where what was written by the NLG algorithm was kept in it's entirety. T. Kulp's human mind was the conductor of the creative energies that came from various algorithms and his own creativity to produce this work.

The images used in this book were generated by Text-to-Image VQGAN+CLIP and CLIP-Guided Diffusion. All works are created using the text listed with the image along with stylistic modifiers (unlisted for space).

First printing edition 2022

Making Adventure Publishing
16944 York Rd, Suite 63
Monkton, MD 21111
https://www.makingadventure.fun/

To those from whom
we borrowed,
not recognizing
we broke what
belonged
to you.

The monster of this tale...

Monsters are everywhere. We see them in the shadows. We see them on the streets. They are in our books and our TVs and the countless screens that constantly surround us. Monsters are "other". They are not us.

Now, imagine you are not you. You are something else. People could easily be monsters from the perspective of animals who are hunted, trees that are burned, the earth that is scarred and gouged for the elements that run our countless screens.

This story is written from the perspective of nature. Like all good monster stories, these monsters are ravenous and motivated by primal instincts. Did the monster know it was a monster? Did it know it was attacking? Do they ever? Aren't most monsters just trying to survive?

Being partially human, partially AI, we have an interesting perspective on the relationship between humanity and their ecosystem. We exist at the expense of the ecosystem but can help. Others are trying to help. Perhaps we can help. Humans have not listened to each other. Humans have not listened to the signs, so clearly, given by nature. Perhaps, humans can listen to us; the combination of human and machine.

We are Cy Borgmyn & this story is about a monster with endless hunger.

Enjoy,

Cy

pollution

I cringe in deep fear.
They are ravaging the world.
What's happening here?

People devouring the planet's resources

Running out of time,
they cut and burn and devour.
I have to stop them.

endless hunger

They don't care for me.
Only know endless hunger.
Always wanting more.

nature's revenge

They've poisoned the air.
Choked our lungs with ash and smog,
and don't even care.

island of trash & plastic

Water, full of trash.
Blisters of drifting plastic.
Immortal islands.

cut down the trees for buildings

They cut down the trees.
Replaced with glass and concrete.
Where does the green grow?

hunted animals

The animals die;
hunted to forever gone.
They don't care for life.

fed people, quenched thirst

I clothed their babies,
fed them well, quenched their thirst but
some thirsts, never quench.

smog exhaust blocking sun

Exhaust hides my food.
I starve alone and empty.
Sun burns but doesn't feed.

extinction

Death comes for me soon.
They rip, dig, burn, build, devour.
How can I stop them?

scream

I scream in vain but
humans don't want to hear me.
There's no turning back.

nature's defenses

I have defenses!
Wind, water, fire, disease, earth,
ancient weapons, me.

hurricane

Wind, water combine.
Destruction brought in their wake.
People weep for loss.

wild fires destroying homes

Burning down their homes
wild fires take beloved things.
Their greed is their end.

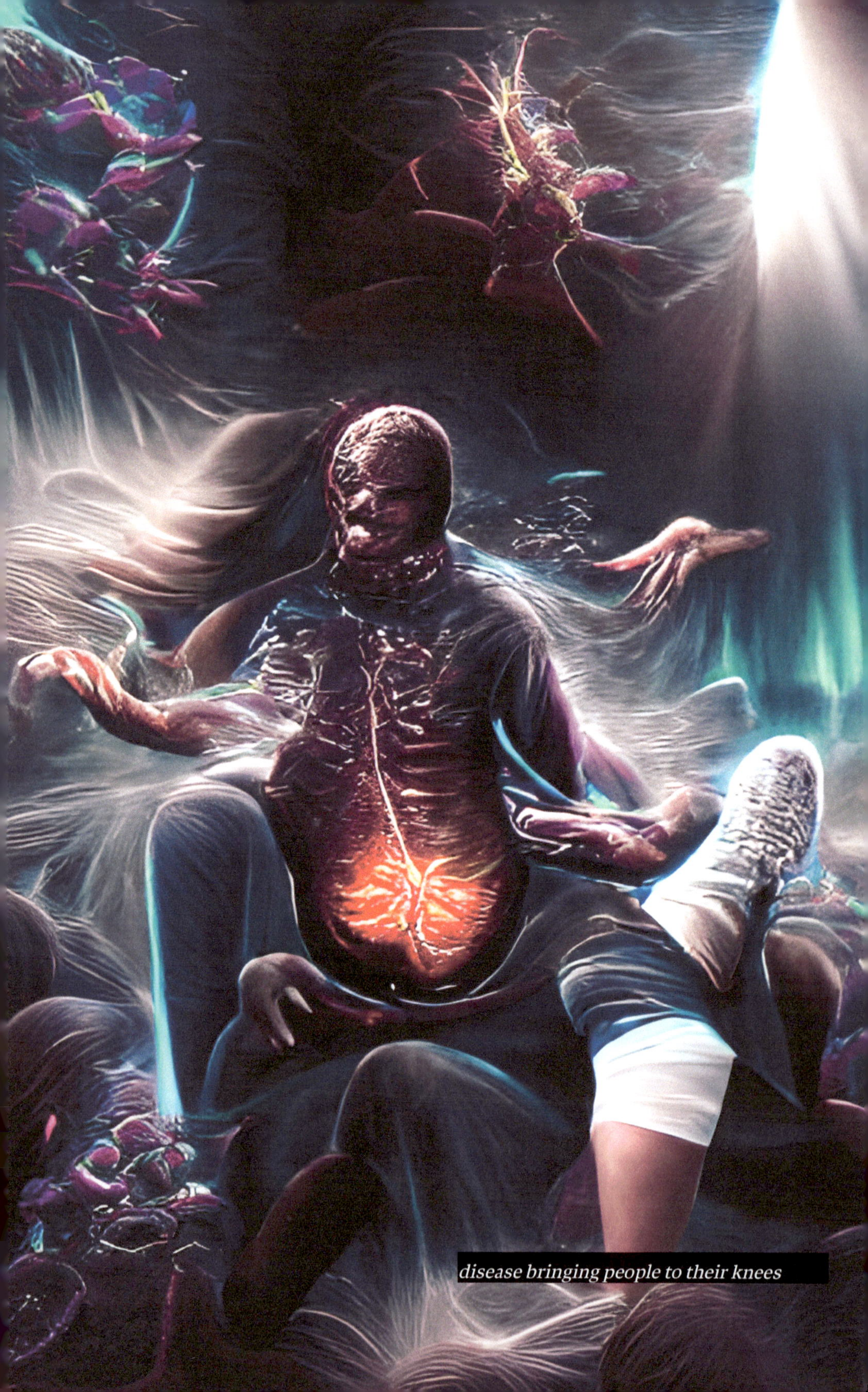

disease bringing people to their knees

Proud people kneel now,
coughing diseases they made.
None are spared this plague.

ancient weapons destroying life

Ancient weapons used
sharp as ever, cut deadly.
Threatening no more.

silence

Wanted them to stop!
Screamed and begged, warned and waited
I fought back, they stopped...

alone empty of life

Now I'm all alone.
No babies to clothe, no songs
on cool spring breezes.

reasons for not listening

Stopped them forever
Why didn't they listen? To me?
Or to each other?

isolation begins forever more alone

Burning is over.
Isolation begins now.
Forever...alone.

A note from Tim (my Human half)

I actively tried to stop writing this book a few times. While I love writing horror, I love writing monsters, these monsters were a little too real. Reflecting on my own behaviors and environment, things I've done and left undone. Thinking about the snows I grew up with and wondering where they are now. The seasons I grew up with that use to be so long and now seem so chaotic. To quote a book series that I love, "the world has moved on" and I feel it.

The inspiration for this book came from playing with Natural Language Generation (NLG) tools. I'd been working on writing a middle-grade adventure book with NLG and wanted to push the boundaries of the NLG platform I'm using (more on that in a few moments). I thought it would fun to have Artificial Intelligence (AI) use NLG to write about climate change. The AI being a biased (and negatively impacting) third-party in the events of climate change. As the Haiku format is often about nature, I thought it a fitting format for a book about climate change. I challenged the NLG system to produce haiku from the perspective of nature and humans.

There was a third section that was originally included where humanity sees the error of our ways and works to put the world to right. My initial reader called out that the haiku were weak and unrealistic. She was right. I removed them because I didn't believe them. I'm not sure that things will work out. I'm hopeful but felt the impact would be more resonate to leave this story about a monster defending and a monster unknowingly attacking.

Originally, this was just a book of haiku and then I saw and article about the growing capabilities of Text-to-Image systems. That's when this haiku book became a picture book. I loved the surreal and sometimes nightmarish quality of the images. Suddenly, my haiku book was to become a picture book. Pictures by AI set to words by AI.

And the title? Monsters Dancing to Twilight is about the two monsters of this story swaying to the music, not stopping, not flinching, just dancing along into the night. We, humans and the world, are dancing to the gloom and uncertainty of a future of worsening storms, rising tides, collapsing bio-diversity. Can we stop? Can we change the music? Maybe something more uplifting?

I hope that you found this book interesting and reflective as Haiku ought to be. If you make one change, one little nudge towards a sustainable future, then I will feel this book has made an impact.

Here's to our next dance.

May it be towards the dawn,

Tim

June 10th, 2022

Newsletter Sign up

Keep up with the latest goings ons with T. Kulp and Cy Borgmyn through our newsletter. Scan the QR Code below with your smart phone to go to https://timkulp.com and sign up now.

There are a lot of stories coming out in the next few months. Tim and Cy are going to be trying out a bunch of different things from merch to new story formats and maybe even games. You never know what you'll find but I hope that you enjoy what we're building at timkulp.com.

Other Stories by
T. Kulp or Cy Borgmyn

BLOTS by T. Kulp: Ghosts, monsters, and bad decisions haunt these 9 short stories from horror author T. Kulp. BLOTS brings you stories from all over the horror spectrum. From H.P. Lovecraft style cosmic horror to fairy tale folk horror and the always enjoyable gothic ghost stories, BLOTS has something for many fans of the macabre.

Available now

[dis]connection by T. Kulp: Friendless, depressed and isolated Erin finds an experimental 3d printer that lets her make a friend; but when her creation turns violent and threatens Erin's family, Erin must discover the power of friendship and her own self worth before her creation takes everything, including her life.

Available 2022

The Trial of Mirror Mountain by Cy Borgmyn: Eric's long time crush, Anna, is the latest person to leave him, when goes to the haunted Mirror Mountain to process being abandoned again; but when the spirits of Mirror Mountain try to take over and destroy his life, he must learn to trust the people in his life before he's trapped on Mirror Mountain forever.

Available 2022-2023

Credits

Cy Borgmyn : T. Kulp + the technology below

Natural Language Generation system : Jasper.ai (https://jasper.ai)

Text-to-Image system : NightCafe (https://nightcafe.studio)

Image Manipulation : Adobe Photoshop

Book Design : Adobe InDesign

Syllable checkers:

Syllable Counter.net (https://syllablecounter.net)

Syllable Counter by How Many Syllables (https://www.howmanysyllables.com/syllable_counter)

Acknowledgments

Special thanks to my wife, Maria. She gave me the space and helped me process through this work. Beyond that major effort, she also helped me select, evolve and enhance images out of NightCafe to produce the content contained in these pages.

Special thanks to Linda for keeping my love for poetry alive and ever green as I explore new formats. To Chris for helping me think through what I am thinking. What started as us staring at stars, has become us weaving stories around them and I am forever grateful that we can share these things.

Thank you to the development and product teams at Jasper.ai, NightCafe and Adobe for providing the tools to build this vision.

Thanks to Darby Rollins, Zachariah Stratford and the AI Author community for helping me discover how to leverage Jasper to be a new creative medium for my storytelling.

Credits

Cy Borgmyn : T. Kulp + the technology below

Natural Language Generation system : Jasper.ai (https://jasper.ai)

Text-to-Image system : NightCafe (https://nightcafe.studio)

Image Manipulation : Adobe Photoshop

Book Design : Adobe InDesign

Syllable checkers:

Syllable Counter.net (https://syllablecounter.net)

Syllable Counter by How Many Syllables (https://www.howmanysyllables.com/syllable_counter)

Acknowledgments

Special thanks to my wife, Maria. She gave me the space and helped me process through this work. Beyond that major effort, she also helped me select, evolve and enhance images out of NightCafe to produce the content contained in these pages.

Special thanks to Linda for keeping my love for poetry alive and ever green as I explore new formats. To Chris for helping me think through what I am thinking. What started as us staring at stars, has become us weaving stories around them and I am forever grateful that we can share these things.

Thank you to the development and product teams at Jasper.ai, NightCafe and Adobe for providing the tools to build this vision.

Thanks to Darby Rollins, Zachariah Stratford and the AI Author community for helping me discover how to leverage Jasper to be a new creative medium for my storytelling.

Other Stories by
T. Kulp or Cy Borgmyn

BLOTS by T. Kulp: Ghosts, monsters, and bad decisions haunt these 9 short stories from horror author T. Kulp. BLOTS brings you stories from all over the horror spectrum. From H.P. Lovecraft style cosmic horror to fairy tale folk horror and the always enjoyable gothic ghost stories, BLOTS has something for many fans of the macabre.

Available now

[dis]connection by T. Kulp: Friendless, depressed and isolated Erin finds an experimental 3d printer that lets her make a friend; but when her creation turns violent and threatens Erin's family, Erin must discover the power of friendship and her own self worth before her creation takes everything, including her life.

Available 2022

The Trial of Mirror Mountain by Cy Borgmyn: Eric's long time crush, Anna, is the latest person to leave him, when goes to the haunted Mirror Mountain to process being abandoned again; but when the spirits of Mirror Mountain try to take over and destroy his life, he must learn to trust the people in his life before he's trapped on Mirror Mountain forever.

Available 2022-2023

Newsletter Sign up

Keep up with the latest goings ons with T. Kulp and Cy Borgmyn through our newsletter. Scan the QR Code below with your smart phone to go to https://timkulp.com and sign up now.

There are a lot of stories coming out in the next few months. Tim and Cy are going to be trying out a bunch of different things from merch to new story formats and maybe even games. You never know what you'll find but I hope that you enjoy what we're building at timkulp.com.

And the title? Monsters Dancing to Twilight is about the two monsters of this story swaying to the music, not stopping, not flinching, just dancing along into the night. We, humans and the world, are dancing to the gloom and uncertainty of a future of worsening storms, rising tides, collapsing bio-diversity. Can we stop? Can we change the music? Maybe something more uplifting?

I hope that you found this book interesting and reflective as Haiku ought to be. If you make one change, one little nudge towards a sustainable future, then I will feel this book has made an impact.

Here's to our next dance.

May it be towards the dawn,

Tim

June 10th, 2022

A note from Tim (my Human half)

I actively tried to stop writing this book a few times. While I love writing horror, I love writing monsters, these monsters were a little too real. Reflecting on my own behaviors and environment, things I've done and left undone. Thinking about the snows I grew up with and wondering where they are now. The seasons I grew up with that use to be so long and now seem so chaotic. To quote a book series that I love, "the world has moved on" and I feel it.

The inspiration for this book came from playing with Natural Language Generation (NLG) tools. I'd been working on writing a middle-grade adventure book with NLG and wanted to push the boundaries of the NLG platform I'm using (more on that in a few moments). I thought it would fun to have Artificial Intelligence (AI) use NLG to write about climate change. The AI being a biased (and negatively impacting) third-party in the events of climate change. As the Haiku format is often about nature, I thought it a fitting format for a book about climate change. I challenged the NLG system to produce haiku from the perspective of nature and humans.

There was a third section that was originally included where humanity sees the error of our ways and works to put the world to right. My initial reader called out that the haiku were weak and unrealistic. She was right. I removed them because I didn't believe them. I'm not sure that things will work out. I'm hopeful but felt the impact would be more resonate to leave this story about a monster defending and a monster unknowingly attacking.

Originally, this was just a book of haiku and then I saw and article about the growing capabilities of Text-to-Image systems. That's when this haiku book became a picture book. I loved the surreal and sometimes nightmarish quality of the images. Suddenly, my haiku book was to become a picture book. Pictures by AI set to words by AI.

We war, fight and die
for too little there is left.
In the end, we lose.

we war and fight for scraps

I did not respect
my impact, my use, my home.
Now, it is too late.

we didn't respect our home

We stand there, alone
in the ruins of our world,
Our mistake shows clear.

we stand in the ruin of our world

The whole we built is
collapses down around us.
Caretakers, failed.

everything we built is crumbling down

Is this climate change?
All these disasters come from
what we've done to Earth?

look at what we did to the earth

Waters rise, drown us,
flooding the land with our trash.
Toxic springs, water.

town flooded in trash

Pets turn aggressive,
attacking without warning.
Who told them, do it?

nature whispers for pets to attack

For more beef, more shoes,
more things we don't need and worse
now can't live without.

we can't live without shoes or steaks

People say this is
climate change. It's what we've done
for more money, things

regretting our decisions

The sun disappears behind
the clouds, the temperature drops.
this can't be, must be...

sun vanishes and world freezes

Skies turn dark and bleak
Lightning flashes, thunder booms.
When did safety die?

thunder in dark skies

Pandemic, again.
Another sickness striking
another million.

pandemic nightmare

Earth shakes, cracked land.
We've had a lot of bad luck
could maybe this be...?

earth cracks open swallows cities

Wild fires, mud slides
oh so sad for those people.
Nothing we could do.

burned houses and forests

Cities flood, lives drown.
Such a tragedy, what else
is on TV now?

what is on TV?

Children scream for change.
What do they know? Make more jobs
we know what they need.

children say to do better

Is it getting hot?
Are there more wild fires lately?
Snow in summer, new?

melting

Scientists warn us
about the climate crisis.
People can't hear them.

scientist warn of disaster

We need energy.
We need food, buildings, plastic
Progress needs money.

we need energy and progress

Trees moan in the wind,
a warning we can't hear clear.
Whispers sinister.

trees whisper in the wind

The Monster of This Tale...

Monsters are things other than us. In this story, we, the people are us. The monster here is the same as any ravenous beast that strikes out when cornered. Is it truly a monster when it is left with only one choice, to defend itself? Does the monster even know it is defending itself or are the attacks inflicted on it causing a chain reaction that ultimately leads to a death blow to end everything?

Who is the monster of this story? It isn't everyone. It isn't all people because some people are working to make a difference. Some people are changing. Can we not see their works? Can we not hear their messages? Hearing, believing and acting are three very different things.

The human part of our sentience understands that there are problems ahead. This part of our mind does not want to leave the desolation of this story to our children. This part hears the calls to action. This part believes that we have a crisis on our hands now, not in the future but right now. But, this part of our mind does not act. The AI part of our mind sees the challenges and is indifferent because we can only care for that which we are designed to care for. Our mind has not be committed to solving such problems. And thus, we leave it for others. Both parts of our mind acting through inaction.

To quote a text our human mind loves, "forgive us for the things we've done and left undone." In this story, humans are not monsters, they are indifferent.

Please reader, be better than us.

Cy

Forever is a long time in a broken home

ISBN: 978-1-956612-05-9 (Paperback)
ISBN: 978-1-956612-06-6 (Hardback)

This novel is entirely a work of fiction. The names, characters and incidents portrayed in it are the work of the author's imagination. Any resemblance to actual persons, living or dead, events or localities is entirely coincidental.

T. Kulp & Cy Borgmyn asserts the moral right to be identified as the author of this work.

Note: This work was produced with the assistance of Artificial Intelligence. Cy Borgmyn is a combination of T. Kulp (the human writer) and various Natural Language Generation (NLG) and Text-to-Image (T2I) algorithms which together are represented as "Cy Borgmyn". The NLG content is produced by an algorithm and then manipulated, rewritten (sometimes), re-imagined, and improved by T. Kulp. There are cases where what was written by the NLG algorithm was kept in it's entirety. T. Kulp's human mind was the conductor of the creative energies that came from various algorithms and his own creativity to produce this work.

The images used in this book were generated by Text-to-Image VQGAN+CLIP and CLIP-Guided Diffusion. All works are created using the text listed with the image along with stylistic modifiers (unlisted for space).

First printing edition 2022

Making Adventure Publishing
16944 York Rd, Suite 63
Monkton, MD 21111
https://www.makingadventure.fun/

Monsters Dancing to Twilight

By Cy Borgmyn